For information about permission to reproduce selections from this book, write to Permissions,
Houghton Mifflin Harcourt Publishing Company, 215 Park Avenue South, New York, New York 10003.

Library of Congress Cataloging-in-Publication Data is on file.

Book design by Stephanie Cooper and Bill Smith Studio

ISBN: 978-0-547-36897-9

www.hmhbooks.com
www.marthathetalkingdog.com

Manufactured in China/LEO 10 9 8 7 6 5 4 3 2 1

Shelter Dog Blues

Adaptation by Jamie White

Based on a TV series teleplay written by Matt Steinglass

Based on the characters created by Susan Meddaugh

HOUGHTON MIFFLIN HARCOURT

Boston • New York • 2010

MARTHA SAYS HELLO

It's me, Martha, here to introduce my story.

Hi there!

If I were any other dog, my introduction might go something like this:

Woof. Woof, woof.

But ever since Helen fed me her alphabet soup, I've been a dog who can speak. And speak and speak . . .

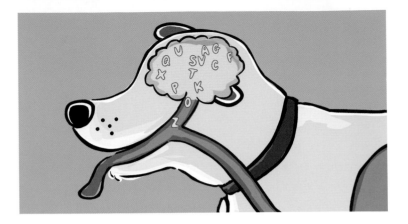

No one's sure how or why, but the letters in the soup traveled up to my brain instead of down to my stomach.

Now, as long as I eat my daily bowl of alphabet soup, I can talk. To my family: Helen, baby Jake, Mom, Dad, and our dog Skits, who only speaks dog. To Helen's best friend, T.D. To anyone who'll listen.

Sometimes my family wishes I didn't talk *quite* so much. But who would want to discourage a talking dog from, well, talking?

Besides, my speaking comes in handy. One night, I called 911 to stop a burglar.

So I guess I'm fortunate. Lucky, that is. But you never know when you might go from lucky to *unlucky*. Last week I found out what it's like to be unlucky and lose the most precious thing of all—freedom.

Sit, stay, and hear all about it . . .

A BUBBLE-NOSED DOG

It all started in the bathroom.

Martha could think of only one good reason to visit the bathroom: to drink from the toilet. But sometimes Martha was dragged to the bathroom against her will.

"You have no right!" Martha yelled, squirming in Helen's arms. "It's not fair!"

"You *have* to take a bath," Helen said. "Get in there!"

Helen began to drop Martha into the soapy water.

"No!" Martha cried. "Not the bubbles! Anything but the—"

SPLASH!

"Bubbles," Martha groaned. She was soaked. "I HATE bubbles! They get in my mouth!"

"If you *ever* stopped talking, that wouldn't happen," Helen said.

"They get up my nose too. Look!" Martha snorted two bubbles into the air.

"Martha, you're fortunate to have a family that gives you a bath when you need one," Helen said.

"Having to do something you hate

doesn't seem very *fortunate* to me," Martha
replied.

"If you knew how many dogs are all alone
in the world, you'd appreciate how lucky you
are."

Helen snapped off Martha's collar. She
hung it on the shower rod so she could scrub
Martha's neck. Outside, a truck rumbled.

"Helen!" Mom called from downstairs. "Did you take out the garbage yet? I hear the truck coming!"

"Be right there!" Helen said. "Lucky dog," she said to Martha. "Just a quick bath today."

Hooray for garbage trucks, Martha thought. She leaped out of the tub.

"So are you fortunate to have to take out the garbage?" Martha asked as Helen dried her off.

"No, but Mom is fortunate she has me to take it out for her," Helen said. "I'd better go."

As soon as Helen left, Martha felt strange. Something was missing, she thought. She looked up at the shower rod.

"Wait," Martha said. "You forgot my collar!"

"I'll get it later!" Helen called.

Humans, Martha thought. *If a dog wants something done right, she has to do it herself.*

Martha jumped onto the edge of the tub and reached for her collar. The tub was slippery. Her paws slid—and *oof!* Martha fell onto her belly.

"It's times like these I wish I had hands," Martha said.

She leaped back onto the tub. But her paws refused to stay put. Martha slipped again.

"ACK!" she cried, grabbing the shower curtain.

This time, Martha took the curtain and rod down with her. They all crashed into the tub.

When Martha's head popped out of the water, she looked like she'd grown a bubble beard. She eyed what had fallen onto the soap dish.

"My collar!" Martha said, grabbing for it. "Whoops!"

Her paw hit the edge of the
dish. The collar shot through
the air and landed on the
windowsill.

"Phew," said Martha. "Safe
and sound."

And that's when her collar
slid right out the window.

THE DOGGONE
DAY BLUES

"NOOOOOO!" Martha cried, looking out the window.

Her collar was in the trash can below. It had fallen on top of a banana peel and a half-eaten hot dog.

Hot dog—yum! Martha thought. *Wait, I can't think about food at a time like this. I have to get that trash can!*

"I WANT THAT GARBAGE! DON'T LET
THEM TAKE IT!" Martha cried. She raced
downstairs.

By the time she got outside, the trash man
was already dumping the garbage into his
truck. He handed the empty can back to Helen.

"GIVE ME THAT TRASH!" Martha yelled.

The truck began to pull away.

"Martha!" said Helen. "Why are you all wet
again?"

"No time for chitchat," Martha said.

13

Helen and Mom watched Martha chase the truck down the street.

"No time to talk?" Helen said. "What's gotten into Martha?"

Mom shook her head. "Chasing after garbage trucks! That dog is acting like a . . . dog! Next thing you know, she'll be drinking from the toilet."

. . . . .

As Helen and Mom watched Martha disappear, the trash man watched Martha grow closer. Covered in bubbles, she was a scary sight. The trash man called Animal Rescue.

"Officer Kazuo here," said the voice at the other end. "Can I help you?"

Kazuo was driving the Shelter Mobile. *BUM, BUM, BADUM* went the radio. People could hear him coming from blocks away.

"An out-of-control dog?" Kazuo said. "*Chasing you? Covered in foam?* Stay away from that dog. I'll be right there!"

Kazuo slammed his foot on the gas. A dog that was foaming at the mouth could have rabies! The Shelter Mobile sped down the street.

Meanwhile, the garbage truck stopped to pick up a dumpster. Martha caught up to it.

"Hold on! My collar is in there!" she yelled. But her voice could not be heard over the sound of the garbage truck.

Why won't he listen to me? Martha wondered. *I'm a talking dog, for crying out loud. If only I could speak to him face to face . . .*

She leaped to his window.

The trash collector still couldn't hear Martha. But he *could* see a crazy-looking dog pop up and down.

"Oh, golly!" he yelled, locking his door.

"Collie? No, I'm looking for my *collar!* That's the thing that goes around my *neck*," Martha said.

The Shelter Mobile screeched to a halt next to her.

"Let's rock and roll," Kazuo said, hopping out. He put on his headphones and crept toward Martha. He held a long stick with a loop at its end.

Oh, good, thought Martha. *Someone to help me.*

"Could you explain to him that I'm searching for my collar?" she asked.

Kazuo walked closer. With his headphones on, he couldn't hear a word Martha said.

"Doesn't *anybody* here understand human?" said Martha. "Hey, what's that stick thing for?"

Kazuo lowered his catch pole.

"Gotcha!" he said.

Before she knew it, Martha was locked in the back of the Shelter Mobile.

She was alone, with no one to hear her. *In this situation, there is only one thing for a dog to do,* she thought.

Martha sang the doggone day blues.

THE DOGGY SLAMMER

It was a sad, lonely ride to the animal shelter. It was also a long time for Martha to go without talking. It was the first thing she did when Kazuo took her out of the Shelter Mobile.

"You don't understand! My collar is lost in the garbage," Martha tried to explain.

It was no use. Kazuo was still wearing his headphones. *BUM, BUM, BADUM,* he hummed.

He carried her to the back of the pound's
reception area. He pressed a button on the wall.
BZZZZ.

A door opened to a room full of cages.
Dogs of all shapes and sizes barked at them.

"In you go!" said Kazuo, shepherding her
into a cage.

Martha looked around her small cell. The
only things in it were an old chew toy and a
bowl of dry dog food.

"What, no burgers?" Martha said. "No chops? Not even a lousy meatball? Maybe I can order in?"

Kazuo left.

"Wait!" Martha cried. "I don't belong here! This is all a big mistake! I *have* a family!"

In the cage next to her, an old bulldog barked. *Ruff, ruff!*

"What do you mean, 'That's what they all say'?" Martha asked.

At home, Helen was worried. She hadn't seen Martha in hours.

"Don't fret," Mom said. "She's been gone longer than this before."

"She'll be back when she's hungry," said Dad. "Martha never misses a meal."

"You don't think she feels neglected, do you?" Helen asked.

"Neglected? *Martha?*" Dad said. "How could she? Neglected dogs are dogs who are forgotten or ignored. You take good care of Martha. You wash her, you groom her—"

"WASH?" Helen cried.

"Oh, no! I just realized something. I never put Martha's collar back on after her bath. She's not wearing her tags!"

"Oh, dear," Mom said. "Let's call the animal shelter."

Dad ran to the phone.

Kazuo was locking up for the night when he heard the telephone ring.

He picked it up and said, "Hello. This is the Animal Rescue Shelter. We're about to close."

"Could you tell me if you picked up a talking dog today?" Dad asked.

"Sir, I can't check the records now, but—" Kazuo narrowed his eyes. "Did you say a *talking* dog?"

"Yes," said Dad. "A dog that can speak. Human language."

"Sir, is this some type of joke?" Kazuo asked.

"Of course not. I'm looking for a talking—"

Click. The phone went dead.

"I guess that's a *no*, then," said Dad.

MARTHA'S SIDE OF THE STORY

So there I was, in the pound. The pooch hooch. The doggy basket of steel.

The place was full of tough dogs who looked like they'd just as soon bite me as sniff me. There was Estelle, the grizzled old poodle;

Wally, the pointer with the chewed-up ear; and Miranda, the cutest Yorkie-poodle you ever saw. (Okay, maybe they weren't *all* so tough.)

Someone growled in the cage next to mine. It was Pops, the bulldog. He was the toughest of them all.

"Sorry, is there a problem?" I asked.

Pops glared at me.

"I'll only be here a day or two," I gulped. "I don't mean to cause any—"

RAAARR! RUFF!

"Oh. My name? I'm Martha," I said. "What's yours?"

"Pops," he barked.

"What are you in for?" I asked.

Pops told me his story. It was rough. He was once a junkyard dog. Pops protected his master's yard like a one-dog burglar alarm. But then his master sold the junkyard, bought a flashy car, and sped off. Poor old Pops was left in the dust. Then there was Miranda in a nearby cage. Her story was sad too. She lived with a rich lady in a big house. She was a good dog. She barked

32

politely. She obeyed every command. Her golden fur perfectly matched the golden colors of the lady's living room. Until the lady changed the room to blue, that is.

"Honey, you don't match the drapes," the lady said one day. And Miranda was tossed into a limo for a one-way ride to Poundsville.

Every dog here was abandoned and alone. Estelle's owners moved to a building where no pets were allowed. And the puppies—Streak, Butterscotch, and Mandarin—never had an owner at all. Or at least they had been brought to the shelter before they could remember.

"I know how you feel," I told them.

Ruff! Ruff! barked Pops.

"What a harsh thing to say," I replied. "Of course I've had it rough. Why, just today, I had to take a . . . *bath!*"

The dogs rolled their eyes.

"With *bubbles!*" I said. "They get in your nose!"

Pops growled.

"Sure, my family will get me in the morning. But I know what it's like to feel unloved," I said. "I was in the shelter when I was a puppy. That's where Helen found me."

They had stopped listening. They had turned their backs. I needed to do something—fast.

"What if I told you I could get us all out of this place?" I said. "Together."

The dogs barked in excitement. Even Pops looked interested.

"Leave it to me," I said. "I have a plan!"

Okay, I thought. *Time to come up with a plan.*

BREAKING AND EXITING

Martha's plan to break out of the shelter had three simple steps:

Step one: Pick up a piece of dog food.

Step two: Flick it at the door's access button.

Step three: If steps one and two don't work, try them again.

Martha didn't really expect to need step three. But she did. She flicked dog food at the button for hours.

The dogs watched pellet after pellet fly by. Some pellets hit the door. Some hit the wall. But even when they hit the button, the door didn't open. Finally, the dogs fell asleep. The only one left watching was a pigeon perched on a cage. And he just shook his head and rolled his eyes.

If I could just figure out how to make something heavier fly across the room, Martha said to herself.

Then she remembered what had started
this whole mess. *My collar flew into the air when
I hit the soap dish,* she thought. *Aha!*

Martha rested the chew toy on her bowl.
She slid the bowl out through the bars of
her cage. Then she slammed her paw onto the
bowl. The chewie whizzed across the room.

Bull's-eye! The door opened with a buzz.

"I DID IT! WE'RE OUT!" Martha cheered, looking around at the dogs. "We're out! We're, uh . . ."

The dogs yawned.

"There must be something I've overlooked," Martha said. "What did I forget?"

Ruff, ruff! Pops barked.

"Er, right," Martha mumbled. "I forgot that we're all inside locked cages."

Martha rattled her door.

"Hey, pigeon!" she called. "Can I get your help down here?"

Coo, coo, said the pigeon.

"What's in it for you?" Martha repeated. "No wonder they call you flying rats!"

The pigeon turned away.

"Wait!" Martha said. "My neighbors keep a twenty-pound bag of birdseed in their garage. You get me out, I'll get you in."

The pigeon swooped down to
Martha's cage. It pushed the door's unlock
button with its head. *Click.* The door
swung open.

"Yippee!" Martha said. "I'm free!"

Martha hurried to open the other cages.
A happy pack of dogs ran into the reception
area. Everyone raced for the exit.

"Now all we have to do is open this last
door," Martha said. "Then we'll be as
free as—*Kazuo?!*"

The dogs skidded to a halt.

"Negative," Kazuo said, walking in with a phone to his ear. "Dog escape is under control. Repeat, dog escape is under control!"

"Well, this is unfortunate timing," Martha said.

Near her, Pops growled.

Pops is so close to freedom, he can smell it,
Martha thought. *Or maybe he smells the Burger
Barn down the street. Mmm, burgers . . . Uh-oh!
Where is Pops going?*

Pops ran under Kazuo's legs and out
the door.

DOGS ON THE RUN

"Hey, Pops! Get back here!" Kazuo called.

Pops was on the run.

So was Martha. She ran out the door, past Kazuo, and down the street. Pops was faster than he looked, but it didn't take her long to catch up with him.

"Stop, Pops! What about the others?" she said.

Suddenly, she heard a *BUM, BUM, BADUM!* Headlights beamed on them from behind.

"Watch out!" Martha said to Pops. "The Shelter Mobile is on our tails!"

"You'll never make it, Pops!" Kazuo shouted.

Pops and Martha raced around a corner.

"This is a dead-end street," Martha said. "Up ahead! He can't follow us there!"

The dogs fled into the woods.

Behind them, the Shelter Mobile screeched to a stop. Kazuo got out to chase them on foot.

"Pops! We're leaving the others behind!"
Martha said. She stopped to catch her breath.
"How can we enjoy being free when we
deserted them—"

Before Martha could finish, she felt
something familiar around her neck. And it
wasn't her collar.

"Gotcha again!" Kazuo said, holding the
catch pole.

"Please," Martha said. "Let Pops go! I
can explain—"

"That's enough from you," Kazuo said.

"You finally hear me?"
Martha asked. "I was beginning
to wonder if you could
only hear music. Or if you
had ears. Or if—"

"Shhh. Did I ask for your opinion?"
Kazuo said. He looked up to see Pops in
the distance. "Pops, what are you doing?"

The old bulldog stood in the moonlight.

"We've been through this before," Kazuo
said softly. "You break out, the world is harsh,
and you feel neglected. Three weeks later,
you're at the shelter again. Come back, Pops.
We'll find you a family."

Pops hung his head. He shuffled toward Kazuo.

"Nice dog," said Kazuo.

Martha watched as Kazuo scratched Pops's head.

Kazuo might not have good ears, Martha thought, *but he has a good heart.*

A NEW DAY

When Martha saw her shelter friends again, it was from behind bars.

Everyone is sad about being back in a cage, Martha thought. *It's all my fault.*

The dogs sulked in silence. The only sound came from the pigeon.

Coo, coo.

"Yes, the birdseed deal is still on!" Martha
snapped. "Jeepers."

Kazuo came in carrying bags of dog food.

"Howdy, boys and girls," he chirped.
"Why the long faces? It's morning. Say hello
to a new day!"

Nobody answered.

"Or not," Kazuo said. "Listen, I know this
place can get gloomy. But I'm trying to find
you families. Escaping doesn't help anybody.
Why don't we make a fresh start?"

He turned to Martha. "Hey, new dog! What kind of chow do you like? Bark once for Meaty Bix, twice for Waggy Wafers."

"My name is Martha," she said. "And I'd like Meaty Bix, please!"

"Let's try this again," said Kazuo. "Bark once for Meaty Bix, twice for Waggy Wafers."

"I don't need to bark. I can talk! Can't I just phone my family so they can bring me home?" Martha asked.

"I'm sorry. Dogs are not allowed to make phone calls," Kazuo replied.

"But you said you hoped we'd find families," Martha said. "I already have one."

"Kid, you have no collar to prove you belong to anyone. If I let you use the phone, then all the dogs will want to."

"Well, didn't anyone call here looking for me?" Martha asked.

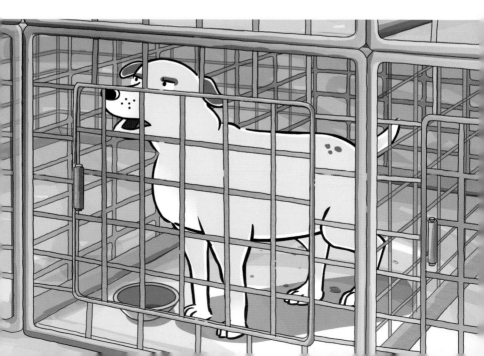

"Oh, yeah. Somebody did call," Kazuo
said, scratching his head. "About a talking dog.
But how do I know you're *that* talking dog?"

"Kazuo!" Martha said.

He sighed. "Okay. What's your number?"

Martha told him. Kazuo began to dial.

"Wait," he said. "What if you're just calling
another talking dog?"

Martha groaned. "Someone is acting like a birdbrain in this room, and it's NOT the pigeon."

"Oh, all right." Kazuo held the phone to Martha's ear.

"Hello?" Helen answered.

"It's me!" Martha said, wagging her tail. "I'm in the animal shelter."

"Martha! Thank goodness! Are you all right?" Helen asked.

"Yes," said Martha.

"That's terrific. I'm so happy," Helen said. "May I ask you something?"

"Sure. What's that?" said Martha.

"WHAT WERE YOU THINKING?" Helen shouted. "WHY DID YOU CHASE STINKY GARBAGE? DO YOU HAVE ANY IDEA HOW WORRIED WE'VE BEEN?"

"Wow," Kazuo said. "Anyone who cares enough to yell that loud has got to be your family."

MARTHA SPEAKS AGAIN

And that's how I busted out of doggy jail.
Kazuo and I waited for my family in the
reception area. It was hard to sit still.

"You have ants in your pants," Kazuo said.

"Kazuo! Dogs do not wear pants," I said.
"Well, unless you count my terrier friend,
Frank. Now, that's just embarrassing.

I mean—"

"Okay, okay," Kazuo said. "Your family will be here soon, Martha. We'll miss you."

"I'll miss you all too. I want to take everyone home with me," I said. "Why is it so hard to find families for the dogs?"

"I guess people don't know about them," Kazuo said.

"I wish we could show everybody how great these dogs are," I said.

Just then, two of my favorite people burst through the door.

"MARTHA!" Helen shouted.

I leaped into Helen's arms. It felt great to be hugged again.

"Thanks for finding our Martha," Mom said to Kazuo. "It will be nice to get her home."

"Oh, I'm not leaving," I said.

"What?" said Helen.

"I've decided I can't abandon my friends. Come meet them!"

I introduced Helen and Mom to the others. The dogs all looked so sad.

"Maybe we could adopt them," Helen said. "They could be part of our family."

Mom shook her head. "That's a lot of dogs."

"And a lot of responsibility," said Kazuo. "I couldn't let you adopt them all unless I knew you could take care of each and every one."

For the first time in my life, I couldn't find any words. At least none that were encouraging.

"How can we get people to adopt the dogs?" Helen asked me as we walked out into the shelter yard.

"They just have to meet them," I said. "Maybe we can sneak the dogs into houses at night. Then when the people wake up—

bingo! They have a dog. It's like Christmas."

"But what if they don't make good families?" Helen said. "Like Kazuo said, people have to want the dogs."

"Right," I said, thinking again.

The faint sound of music interrupted my thoughts. It was the theme song to my favorite TV talent show.

"Hey, we're missing *International Icon*," I said.

"Who cares?" Helen said.

"Only everybody," I said. I call to vote for my favorite contestant every week. "Who can resist great talent?"

Helen's face lit up.

"A dog talent show!" we said together.

It was a great idea, if I do say so myself.

"We can have it right here at the shelter tomorrow," I said. "You spread the word. I'll get the dogs ready. I can't wait to see the looks on their faces when I tell them!"

. . . . .

I told the dogs our idea and waited for their
applause. And waited . . .

This was not the reaction I had imagined
—no reaction.

"Just give it a shot," I said. "I can't promise
anything. But with everyone's help, we can
make this show a success. It's not going to be
easy. It's going to be work, work, and more
work. But you can do it!"

The dogs stood a little straighter. They were listening, and I didn't have to offer any of them a single doggy treat.

"You're going out there dogs," I said, "and you're coming back . . . Well, you'll still be dogs. But YOU'LL HAVE FAMILIES!"

The dogs barked cheerily.

Except for one. Pops grunted and went back to sleep.

BEST PAW FORWARD

Helen and her best friend, T.D., delivered flyers to every dogless kid in town.

They went to all kinds of houses—small, big, neat, and messy. They visited a noisy house of triplets who didn't like to share. And the quiet apartment of a boy who traveled a lot.

"Come see Wagstaff City's Top Dog," Helen said to the boy. "It's the best dog show ever."

"If you're lucky, you'll take home a pet of your own," T.D. added.

The boy frowned. "My parents say it'd be too hard to take a dog on a plane with us."

It seemed like everyone had an excuse for not getting a dog. But Helen and T.D. promised them a show they'd never forget.

· · · · ·

Back at the shelter, Martha was giving the dogs their first lesson in being irresistible.

"Put your best paw forward," she told them. "Let's show the people what makes you, you. Streak, Butterscotch, and Mandarin, what do you do best?"

The puppies stared blankly. They were young and didn't understand Martha's instructions.

"You're affectionate. Show me!"

Yip, yip, yip! they all yipped together.

"QUIET!" Martha said. "Loud yipping is not being affectionate."

Yap? Streak asked.

"Being affectionate means being friendly and showing people you love them," Martha answered. "You know how to do that, right?"

The puppies pounced on Martha and covered her with kisses.

"Okay! A little less affection . . . and drool," Martha said.

Martha turned to Wally, the pointer. "Show me your best quality, Wally!"

He ran to a puddle.

What kind of talent do we have here? Martha wondered.

Wally dropped and rolled. He was a muddy mess. Then he trotted back and shook his coat. Mud splattered onto everyone.

"Maybe we need to review what I meant when I said best quality," said Martha, shaking herself off. "No one comes to the shelter saying, 'Give me your dirtiest dog.' People want clean. They want cute. They want . . . *the low wiggle.*"

The dogs looked confused.

"You don't know what the low wiggle is?" Martha said. "It works like this. When someone comes into the shelter—POW! You turn on the charm. Watch me."

Martha smiled and wagged her tail.

"This is how to say, 'I like you! I hope you like me.' Then you crouch low to the ground and wiggle toward the person. See?" Martha wiggled with her rear in the air.

"For the big finish, show your belly!" Martha flopped onto her back. "Now you try."

The dogs ran in circles. Some crashed into each other. A few skipped the wiggle and went straight for the belly move.

"This is going to take a lot of work," Martha muttered. She looked at Pops, alone in the corner. "Pops, how about you?"

Pops just walked away.

Maybe you can't teach an old dog new tricks, Martha thought. *But I will try. I'll get this ragtag bunch ready for tomorrow's show if it takes me all day.*

Sure enough, Martha was still talking after the sun set. "Eyes, ears, and tails! Come on! I want to see wagging!"

It was a long night.

TOP DOG

The next day, the dogs couldn't believe how many people had come to see them.

"Look at this crowd!" Helen said. "We're sure to get the dogs adopted."

"Don't get your hopes too high," Dad said. "Kazuo has been trying for a long time."

At last, the show was about to begin.

Martha made her grand entrance.

"Welcome to Wagstaff City's Top Dog! I'm your host, Martha. It's time for this show to go to the dogs!"

The dogs strutted down the stage as if it were a runway.

"Awwww!" said the crowd, enjoying the show already.

"Do you want a dog who is always your friend no matter what?" Martha said. "Well, dogs don't come any more loyal than Wally!"

Wally came out wearing his most
loyal look.

"He is so loyal, he nearly lost an ear
protecting his last owner from a bear!"

Wally showed off his chewed-up ear. The
crowd gasped.

"Is that true?" T.D. asked Helen.

"Mostly," Helen said, "NOT."

"I know we travel a lot, but could we *please*
adopt him, Dad?" asked a boy.

"I don't know," said the boy's dad. "How would we take him with us?"

"*Psst*, Wally," Helen whispered. She held an animal carrier. Wally marched inside and shut the door behind him.

"A frequent flyer dog for the family on the go!" Helen said.

"That's the dog for us!" said the boy's dad.

"YES!" said the boy, hugging his father.

Then Estelle pranced onto the stage.

"She's elegant! She's stylish! But is she devoted?" Martha said, looking at a girl in the audience.

"If *devoted* means someone who's going to love you forever, then that's Estelle!"

Estelle did a perfect low wiggle.

"And a poodle won't get hair on your chair," Martha said to the girl's mom.

The mom nodded to her daughter.

"Woo-hoo!" cheered the girl. Estelle leaped into her arms.

Butterscotch trotted out next. She nuzzled Martha's leg.

"What does every human dream of in
a dog?" Martha said. "Affection! As you can
see, Butterscotch is the most affectionate—
HEY!"

One of the triplets yanked Butterscotch off
the stage.

"You're mine," she said, kissing the
puppy's ear.

"She's mine!" yelled her sister.

"No, mine!" yelled the other.

"Please stop fighting! There's more where she came from," Martha said.

Streak and Mandarin came out. The girls scooped them up.

"We're so happy," the triplets said, holding their new pets.

"Me too," said their dad, holding his head.

By the end of the show, each dog had found a family. Or so Martha thought.

"Thanks for coming," she said. "You'll find adoption forms in—"

"Martha, you forgot someone," Helen whispered loudly. She pointed to the stage steps, where Pops sat alone.

"Oops," said Martha. "Pops, do you want to come up here too?"

Pops snuffled, hesitating.

"We have one last contestant," Martha told the crowd. "Give a big paw . . . I mean *hand* for Pops!"

Pops advanced onto the stage.

"Pops may look fierce, but he's as loyal and affectionate as any dog here. Would anyone like to take him home?" Martha asked as the people stood to leave.

"Anyone?" she asked again. But everyone was heading toward the door.

Poor Pops, Martha thought. *He'll feel lonelier than ever.*

Pops began to walk off the stage when a voice stopped him.

"*I'll* adopt him," someone said.

Martha spun around. "Kazuo?"

"Pops, you and I go back a long time," said Kazuo. "What do you say, old guy? Will you be my dog?"

Pops scowled.

Come on, Pops, Martha thought. *Say yes.*

Pops's grumpy face broke into a huge smile. He licked Kazuo's cheek. "Hooray!" the remaining crowd cheered.

"Sealed with a slobbery kiss!'" Martha said. "It looks like my work here is done."

MARTHA SAYS GOODBYE

My shelter friends love their new families. Kazuo is still hosting talent shows. I hear Pops is even introducing the low wiggle to new dogs. I guess you *can* teach an old dog new tricks!

As for me, I went from being lucky to *unlucky* back to lucky again.

Well, that's my story.

Now I'm the same fortunate dog I used
to be. *Un*fortunately, I've ended up in the
same place where this story began.
The bathroom.

Still, it's good to be home
with my chewies, soup, and
most of all, family. Yes,
I love everything about
my home.

Well, almost everything . . .
I still HATE baths.

Uh-oh. I see bubbles. Time
to *gooooooooooooooooooo!*

GLOSSARY

How many words do you remember from the story?

abandon: to leave behind or give up

adopt: to make someone a part of one's family

adore: to love and admire

affectionate: friendly, loving

deserted: left behind or given up by others

devoted: dedicated, loyal

fortunate: lucky in life

loyal: faithful to someone no matter what

neglected: not cared for properly, forgotten

overlooked: forgotten, missed, or ignored

unfortunate: unlucky

Adopting a Dog

Congratulations on deciding to make a dog a part of your family! Remember to make adoption your first option! There are wonderful dogs in shelters across the country, waiting for a second chance to become a family member.

Here are some things to consider:

- Think long-term—your pet can be with you ten to fifteen years from now.
- Do you want a "go-getter," a "goofball," or a "couch potato"? Let the shelter staff help you make the best match for your family.
- Stock up on supplies before you bring your new pet home—shelter staff can guide you on what to get at the pet supply store or supermarket.
- Make sure you can set aside time each day for your dog. Create a family chart for doggy care duties.
- Dog-proof your home: for example, tuck electrical cords out of the way and make sure small toys and poisonous chemicals and plants are out of reach.
- The adult pets at the shelter can be a perfect choice— their sizes and personalities are fully developed, and most are already housebroken!
- Teach your dog good manners. The teaching process will bring you closer together, and a well-behaved pet will make you both happier!

You can visit **www.aspca.org/adoption/** for more details on the adoption process and to find a shelter near you.

ASPCA
WE ARE THEIR VOICE®

Adoption tips provided courtesy of the American Society for the Prevention of Cruelty to Animals.

Don't miss these

MARTHA SPEAKS

adventures:

Chapter book   Picture book

Early readers